I Want to Be an Astronaut   by Byron Barton

HarperCollinsPublishers

I Want to Be an Astronaut. Copyright © 1988 by Byron Barton. All rights reserved. Printed in Mexico. Library of Congress Cataloging-in-Publication Data: Barton, Byron. I want to be an astronaut. Summary: A young child wants to be an astronaut and goes on a mission into space.   [1. Astronautics—Fiction] I. Title. PZ7.B2848Iwa 1988   [E]   87-24311   ISBN 0-694-00261-5   ISBN 0-690-04744-4 (lib. bdg.) ISBN 0-06-443280-7 (pbk.)

I want to be an astronaut,

a member of the crew,

and fly on the shuttle

into outer space.

I want to be up there

on a space mission

and have ready-to-eat meals

and sleep in zero gravity.

I want to put on a space suit

and walk around in space

and help fix a satellite

and build a factory in orbit.

I want to be up there awhile

and then come back to Earth.

I just want to be an astronaut

and visit outer space.